Steve Hartley is many things: author, astronaut, spy, racing-car driver, trapeze-artist and vampire-hunter. His hobbies include puddle-diving and hamster-wrestling and he was voted 'Coolest Dude of the Year' for five years running by *Seriously Cool* magazine. Steve is 493 years old, lives in a golden palace on top of a dormant volcano in Lancashire and never, EVER, tells fibs. You can find out more about Steve on his extremely silly website: www.stevehartley.net

Books by Steve Hartley

The DANNY BAKER RECORD BREAKER series

The World's Biggest Bogey

The World's Awesomest Air-Barf

The World's Loudest Armpit Fart

The World's Stickiest Earwax

The World's Itchiest Pants

The World's Windiest Baby

The Wibbly Wobbly Jelly Belly Flop

The OLIVER FIBBS series

Oliver Fibbs: Attack of the Alien Brain

Oliver Fibbs and the Giant Boy-Munching Bugs

Oliver Fibbs and the Abominable Snow Penguin

Oliver Fibbs and the Clash of the Mega Robots

www.stevehartley.net

OLIVER FIBBS
AND THE CLASH OF THE MEGA ROBOTS

STEVE HARTLEY

ILLUSTRATED BY BERNICE LUM

MACMILLAN CHILDREN'S BOOKS

First published 2014 by Macmillan Children's Books
a division of Macmillan Publishers Limited
20 New Wharf Road, London N1 9RR
Basingstoke and Oxford
Associated companies throughout the world
www.panmacmillan.com

ISBN 978-1-4472-2032-9

135798642

A CIP catalogue record for this book is available from
the British Library.

Printed and bound by CPI Group (UK) Ltd, Croydon CR0 4YY

I'M OLIVER

Hi! I'm Oliver Ranulph Templeton Tibbs, mild-
mannered comic-reader
and **EHTREME
PIZZA-EATER.**
Also known as Oliver
'Fibbs', just because
I tell people I'm
DABMAN, the Daring and Brave, dashing and bold
DEFENDER OF PLANET EARTH (D.O.P.E.).

Meet my Super And Special family:

Mum, Charlotte Pomeroy Templeton Tibbs,
is a life-saving brain surgeon.

Dad, Granville Fitzwilliam Templeton Tibbs, is an award-winning architect.

My big twin sisters, Emma Letitia and Gemma Darcy Templeton Tibbs, go to the National Ballet Academy: ballet, ballet, ballet – it's all they talk about.

Then there's my little brother, Algy – Algernon Montgomery Templeton Tibbs. He's

a maths genius, chess champion and King of Sneakiness.

And how could I forget Constanza, our Italian nanny? She's a bit dizzy, but she gets me.

At school, I've got my best friend Peaches Mazimba on my side. She's the most sensible person *ever*, so I've recruited her to be a D.O.P.E. like me: she's `Captain Common Sense'.

Unfortunately, I've got the Super And Special Gang against me:

Bobby Bragg can break bricks in half with his bare

hands. Aka `the Show-off', he has the Power to **BORE PEOPLE STIFF.**

Hattie Hurley is a Spelling Bee Cheerleading Champion. Aka `the Spell Queen', she has the Power of **Big Words.**

Toby Hadron is a science whizz. Aka `the Boffin', he has the Power of Inventing **REALLY SCARY STUFF.**

And finally there's my teacher, Miss Wilkins, Keeper of the ᏚᎻᏆᏁᎬ ᎢᏆᎷᎬ Points, and dispenser of detentions, especially when she thinks I'm telling *FIBS* – but as I keep telling her (and everyone else): they're not *FIBS*, they're stories!

CHAPTER 1

CYBER-FAIL!

The **robot**'s red eyes blazed into life. Yellow and white lights flickered and flashed across the bulging metal chest as electricity surged and sparked along the tangle of wire nerves inside. Plastic arteries throbbed as oil and water pulsed through them, pumping energy and power into gleaming limbs. Wheels whirred and cogs clicked as the android's head slowly swivelled to stare at its creator: me.

'Yessssssssssssssssssss!' I cried, punching the air. 'I've done it! The **robot** *actually* works!' I lifted the metre-tall metal man carefully off the desk and placed him upright on my bedroom floor. 'This is *soooooooooo* cool.'

My little brother, Algy, stood eye to eye with the **robot**. 'It doesn't look like a toy,' he said, his voice full of awe. 'It looks . . . alive!'

I nodded. 'This Construct-a-Bot kit is the best thing Mum and Dad have ever bought me.'

'What about the Atom-Splitter Home Laboratory chemistry set?' said Algy.

I shot him a fierce look. `Don't mention the chemistry set.´

`But it was exciting having all those firemen in the house.´ A naughty Dr Devious-style grin spread across his face. `And what about the Wonder-Wok Chinese cookery course they sent you on?´

`I poisoned the twins.´

Algy gave a dastardly chuckle. `I know.´

I laughed and pressed a button on the remote control. `Let's see what this **robot** can do.´

Algy began to giggle. `It's doing a pee!´

A trickle of yellow fluid dribbled down the **robot**'s leg and formed a spreading puddle at its feet.

`I don't think that's supposed to happen,´

I said, checking the instruction booklet. `The **Zybot Z99** can walk, talk and shoot rubber rockets from its arms, but it doesn't say anything in here about going to the toilet. One of the hydraulic pumps must be leaking.´

`What's that smell?´ asked Algy, sniffing the air.

Wispy white smoke drifted up from the **robot**'s bottom. My brother's eyes widened and he opened his mouth to say something else.

`No,´ I said quickly. `It doesn't do *that* either.´

The Zybot made loud fizzing, popping sounds. It began to perform a weird jerky dance, lurching backwards and forwards, head swivelling, arms whirling like propellers.

I pressed the red OFF button on the remote control again and again, but the **robot**'s barmy bopping just became even more **FRANTIC.** The Zybot was out of control!

It marched across the bedroom floor towards Algy, growling, `DESTROY! DESTROY!` Thin beams of red light zipped from its eyes. A rubber rocket blasted from its right arm and fizzed past my brother's head.

Algy backed away into a corner of the room as the terrifying toy closed in on him.

`Stop it, Ollie! Save me!` he cried.

In a flash, I remembered what had happened at the end of my new comic, *Agent Q and*

the REVENGE OF THE ROBOTS. My hero was guarding a special meeting of world leaders. Just as President O'Bandana reached out to shake hands with President Putty ...

THE ROBOT SHOOTS A BEAM OF LETHAL MEGA-QUANTUM PARTICLES AT Q.

Now I knew how to save my brother from my faulty Zybot.

Algy had his loaded water pistol in my bedroom, ready to ambush our sisters, Emma and Gemma, when they came home from ballet school that evening. I snatched the gun from the windowsill, and squirted the maniac **robot**.

The toy made a coughing, whining, crackling sound, and smoke billowed out from every nook and cranny in its body. It staggered to a halt, arms frozen in mid whirl. With a deafening **POP**, the head pinged into the air like a party-popper and landed with a thump on the floor at Algy's feet.

We stared at the soaking, smoking ruins of the **robot**.

'Mum and Dad won't be happy,' remarked my brother, gingerly prodding the Zybot's head with his foot.

'Just because I fixed Dad's glasses doesn't mean I'm going to be an amazing mechanical engineer,' I said.

'But you know what they're like – they're desperate to find something you're **BRILLIANT** at apart from fibbing.'

'I don't tell *FIBS*, Algy – I tell stories.' My

shoulders sagged, and I flopped down onto my bed. 'I was going to take the Zybot to **SHOW AND TELL** at school tomorrow morning. It would've been spectacular.'

I held my head in my hands. **SHOW AND TELL** was going to be PAIN AND TORTURE again. My arch-enemy, Bobby Bragg, leader of the **SAS** (Super And Special) **KIDS**, was going to have a field day. I could hear his mocking voice in my head: `You're a **DAB KID**, Tibbs – **Dull And Boring!**

Dead And Buried, more like.

CHAPTER 2

THE NEW KID

The next morning, our nanny, Constanza, drove us to our schools, shouting angrily in Italian at the other drivers on the road, while the twins twittered on about *tours* and *temps* and *sous sous* (whatever they are), and Algy played chess on his computer. I just stared out of the window, wondering what I could do to escape my fate.

WHAT IF... Constanza drove through a

time portal, and we found ourselves monkey-rustling with my ancestor, the notorious pirate Black Jack Tibbs?

Or, **WHAT IF** . . . a black hole had appeared under the school and sucked it to another part of the universe, so we all got the day off?

Or **WHAT IF** . . .

Constanza braked to a halt outside my school gates. I sighed. It was still here: no time portal, no black hole. My best friend, Peaches, met me in the playground, and even though it was warm and sunny she was wearing a plastic raincoat.

'It said on the weather forecast that it might rain,' she explained when she saw my puzzled look. 'So I put this on, just in case. Did you finish your Zybot?'

'Yes,' I said, pulling the **robot**'s head from my bag to show her. 'Honest, Pea, it would have been the best **SHOW AND TELL** *ever*. There was no way Bobby Bragg could have made fun of me. But the **robot** went berserk and attacked Algy, so I squirted it with water and it exploded.' I held up the smoke-stained head. 'This is all I've got to show.'

When we got into class, there was a boy standing next to Miss Wilkins. Everyone stared at him, like they always do with new kids, but he didn't look away, or look down at his feet, or move closer to the teacher – he just stared back at them, like he wasn't new at all, like he'd been in the class for years. I couldn't help staring either; this kid was *different* – his smart clothes, his long hair, the way he stood with his

hands casually shoved into his trouser pockets . . .

'We have a new addition to our class,' said Miss Wilkins when we'd all settled down at our tables. 'I'd like to introduce Zoot Zipparolli, who will be joining us until the end of summer term. Zoot is Bobby Bragg's cousin.'

Everyone turned to look at Bobby, who leaned back in his chair, his arms folded, smiling at Zoot.

I groaned quietly. *Oh no, I thought, not another Bragg to deal with.*

'Now then, Zoot,' continued Miss Wilkins. 'Normally we do **SHOW AND TELL** on a Monday morning, and as your last name begins with Z, you should go last. However, I think everyone would like to know a bit more about you, so, just this once, why don't you go first?'

Zoot shrugged. 'Sure, no problem,' he said. His accent was American, but with a bit of Italian mixed in, like Constanza's. 'My dad's

Antonio Zipparolli, the famous film director. He's in town filming a new spy thriller starring George Looney.'

Everyone – including me – went, 'Ooooooooooo.'

'When the filming's done, we'll be leaving for Australia to shoot his next film,' continued Zoot. 'That's why I'm only here for a few weeks.'

'So where do you live?' asked Melody Nightingale.

'We have a home in Los Angeles.'

'Is it magnificent, gargantuan and

luxurious?´ asked Hattie Hurlie, who was a National Cheerleading Spelling Bee Champion, and loved using **Big Words.**

`It´s big and fancy, if that´s what you mean,´ laughed Zoot. `But I don´t get to see it much. I´m usually travelling around the world from place to place with my mom and dad.´

The class gave out a low, whispered, `W o w w w w !´

`How **exciting**!´ said Miss Wilkins. `Have you actually *met* George Looney?´

Zoot nodded. `I´ve known him all my life. I call him ˝Uncle George˝. He´s a pal.´

`Is it true what all the gossip magazines are saying, that he´s going out with Ritzy Savoy, the famous actress?´ Miss Wilkins gushed.

Zoot frowned and laughed. `I don´t know

anything about *that* kind of stuff.'

This new kid was definitely Super And Special, but then I realized what was *different* about him: he was the coolest person I'd ever met; he was almost as cool as my hero, *Agent Q!*

Miss Wilkins's face went red and she sighed. 'George Looney's my favourite film star.' She stared into space for a few seconds, sighed again, then pointed to the empty chair next to Bobby. 'Zoot, why don't you sit next to your cousin?'

Bobby gave Zoot a playful punch on the arm as he took his place, looking around the classroom, grinning at us all.

It was time for **PAIN AND TORTURE** Time to begin properly and as usual the Super And Special

Kids had all got amazing things to talk about.

Bobby told everyone he'd got through to the county 100 metre finals, and that if he won he'd go on to the Regional Championships. He showed us a newspaper clipping about him headed: `Local Boy in a Hurry!´

`How promising!´ said Miss Wilkins. `Let's hope you win.´

Toby Hadron showed us a jam jar full of thick, **slimy green** liquid. A sticker on the jar said, `Primordial Soup´. I thought he was going to talk about his lunch, but I was wrong.

`This mix of chemicals is what scientists think the first life on Earth came from,´ he told us, staring intently at the sticky goo. `All I need to do is pass a million volts of electricity through it, and there's a sixty-three point five per cent chance I'll make new life.´

`How dangerous!´ exclaimed Miss Wilkins.

`You're going to need a lot of batteries,´ laughed Jamie Ryder.

Hattie Hurley had made a giant word-search puzzle, made up entirely of strange animal names like `axolotl´, `bandicoot´ and `dromedary´.

`This is just the first,´ she said. `I'm going to do a new one every week.´

`How useful!´ enthused Miss Wilkins. `We can all do the puzzles in literacy!´

Melody Nightingale was a **BRILLIANT** singer,

and was always being asked to perform at big events. This time, she'd been given a part in a big science-fiction musical on stage in London: *RETURN TO THE FLEA-BITTEN PLANET*. She sang a slow, soppy song from the show called, `**EVERY ROBOT NEEDS A HUG**´.

`How beautiful,´ sighed Miss Wilkins.

The rest of us – the *DAB* (**Dull And Boring**) *KIDS* – did our best.

Leon Curley showed us his new haircut.

`How cool!´ said Miss Wilkins. (I'm not sure if she meant that she liked it, or that his hair was now so short he'd get cold ears?)

Millie Dangerfield told us a sparrow had pooped on her head outside the BestCo supermarket, and showed us the photograph her mum had taken.

When everyone laughed, Miss Wilkins said, `How lucky!´

Peaches showed us the dog collar she'd made from an old leather belt.

`But you haven't got a dog,´ called out Bobby Bragg.

`No,´ replied Peaches, `but if I do get one I won't have to buy a collar.´

`How sensible!´ said Miss Wilkins.

When it was my turn to stand up in front of the class, I held up the Zybot's head.

`I built a **robot**,´ I said.

`It'd work better if it had a body,´ shouted Bobby, nudging Zoot and laughing.

I thought about what had happened when I'd

pressed the button on the remote control. The words tumbled out of my mouth before my brain had chance to say, `Don't do it, Ollie!'

WHAT IF...

`When we bought the robot, we were tricked by the shopkeeper, who was actually the twisted criminal Tarquin Doombringer in disguise,' I told the class. `This Construct-a-Bot kit was supposed to be a **Zybot Z99**, but he sold me a **Devilbot X21** instead. As soon as I turned on the power, the evil android began attacking my little brother, Algy – aka Dr Devious.'

I noticed Zoot staring at me open-mouthed. Bobby whispered something in his ear and the new kid smiled.

Miss Wilkins sighed. `Oliver, we really haven't got time for one of your Daring And Brave flights of fancy . . .'

`There's not much more to tell, miss,' I replied. `As the deadly machine began firing rockets and laser beams at Algy, I pulled out my special *DAB*MAN pen, took aim and zapped its metal head off.'

I tossed the **robot**'s head in the air like a football and caught it. `The world is safe again.'

`How reassuring,' said Miss Wilkins. (I think she was being sarcastic). `Is there *any* chance that one day you might do a *normal* SHOW

AND TELL? Write this down as extra homework.´

`But, miss,´ I protested. `The **robot** really did attack Algy, and I really *did* save him.´

As I slunk back to my seat, I heard Bobby Bragg sing, `Liar! Liar! Pants on fire!´

I sat back down next to Peaches and she tutted and shook her head. `Will you never learn?´

`Before we start lessons I have an announcement to make,´ said Miss Wilkins when **SHOW AND TELL** was over. `As you know, the school has been given money to improve our library. We've ordered lots of new books and equipment, like computers, printers, a copying machine and a paper shredder. A lot of work needs doing to organize and run the new library, and I'd like to ask Peaches if she'd help me do it.'

The class turned to stare at Peaches, who had a smile so wide it seemed too big for her face.

'Me, miss?' she said. 'I'd like to be a librarian when I grow up.'

'It's a very important job, and I can't think of anyone better to do it,' added Miss Wilkins as she presented Peaches with a shiny badge that said, 'Library Monitor'.

As the class applauded and Bobby Bragg yawned, I shouted, `YAY! GO, PEA!´

For the rest of the day, Bobby acted like he owned Zoot, taking him around the school, showing him off to the other kids and teachers. `This is my cousin, Zoot. He's famous. He knows George Looney.´

At lunchtime, Bobby, Zoot and the other Super And Special kids made a grand entrance into the dining hall. `Make way for the **SAS VIPS**,´ called Bobby, clearing a way through the kids queuing for lunch.

As usual, I sat with Peaches and watched as she gobbled down her food.

`I know it's not sensible to eat so fast, but I need to hurry,´ she said between mouthfuls of apple pie and custard. `I want to start

27

working in the new library.'

There was a burst of laughter from the Super And Special kids' table. Zoot was sitting there with Bobby, Toby and Hattie. He even managed to look cool eating spaghetti Bolognese, separating out the thin strands of pasta, curling them expertly on his fork and getting them into his mouth without slopping a single drop of sauce down his shirt.

`I wish I was cool like Zoot,´ I said.

Peaches smiled. `And I bet he wishes he could have custard on the end of his nose.´ She handed me a napkin. `Just like you.´

CHAPTER 3

BIG BOOKS

'I've *got* to get this working,' I said to Algy that night as I screwed the Zybot's head back on to its body. 'I'm fed up with being **Dull And Boring.** I want to be as cool as the King of Coolovia, the coolest country on the continent of Cool.'

I didn't say it to Algy, but I what I was really thinking was that I want to be as cool as Zoot.

I took the metal plate off the **robot**'s chest and we stared at the tangle of singed wires and soggy rubber tubes inside. They looked nothing like the neat and tidy diagram in the instruction manual.

Algy whistled and shook his head. 'It's a **big** job,' he said. 'I can't help you right now because I've got to study for my exams. If you can't fix it, can I have a go when I've finished them?'

I fiddled here and tweaked there, but nothing seemed to work. The Zybot's eyes stayed dark, and his metal body didn't even twitch. In the end I gave up, plonked the **robot** in Algy's room and went to bed.

The next morning, I got to school and found Peaches had already been working in the library for over an hour. At morning break I went to see how she was getting on at her new job.

She was busy using the new super-duper

copier machine, copying pictures and posters
and sticking them up on the walls of the library.
She was as happy as The Chuckler, the diabolical
prankster in *Agent Q and the Funny-
bone Fiasco*, after he'd started a war between
the nations of Flyova and Jumpova.

'If you want to help, you can shred that pile
of paper,' she said.

She stuck a
picture of the school
hamsters, Rambo,
Rocky and Rooney,
over the shredder.

'Zoot's nice,'
said Peaches, picking
up a book that someone had left on a table.
She headed for the bookshelves to put it in its

DON'T THROW IT!
SHRED IT!
WE NEED TO SNUGGLE AND
SNOOZE IN A BED
OF SHRED!

proper place. `He came in here at home-time yesterday. He took out a huge book about Australia. He said he wanted to learn about the next country he was going to visit.´

`I've not spoken to him yet,´ I said. `He hangs out with Bobby most of the time, and he's so super-cool.´

`I thought he'd be just like Bobby,´ said Peaches. `But he's not. You should speak to him.´

`He wouldn't want to talk to me . . .´

I didn't say any more, because Peaches had growled, and stomped a few paces down the aisle of books. `Why would someone put a book by Ronald Durl next to one by Kay Jay Howling? Don't people know their alphabet?´ She placed her fists on her hips and studied the rows of books. `In fact, they're *all* out of order,´ she said.

34

'This library needs organizing *now*, before the new books arrive.'

I turned and headed for the door, but I wasn't fast enough.

'Oh no you don't, Ollie,' she said. 'We're going to pull every book off the shelves and put them in neat piles on the floor: one pile for authors with last names beginning with A, another for B, another for C, and so on right through the alphabet.'

'But ... but ... I said I'd help Leon sharpen his pencils,' I replied.

'Leon Curley can sharpen his own pencils – we've got work to do.'

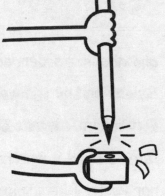

A.CORKIN-BOTTLE
CHRIS CROSS
LOWDEN CLEAR
ORSON CARTE
DAISY CHAIN
JUSTIN CASE
ALPHA BOOT
PEARL BUTTON
TIM BURR
TERRI BULL
ROSE BUSH
PIXIE BOTT
TED E. BEAR
MACK ARONI
AIREY ARM-PITT
PHIL AGAP
B. ARKIN-MADD
TOM ATTABOY
D. ANGLES-DOWN

Pea was like a girl on a mission. Soon, the shelves were empty, and we had a long row of wobbly book-stacks, like crooked tree stumps growing out of the library floor. Every break she grabbed me and hauled me into the library to put the books in each stack into perfect alphabetical order, doing a few letters each day. By the end of the week, I knew what *Agent Q* felt like in *Agent Q and the TIME TINKERERS*, when he was lured into a time vortex by Tempus Tinker, and forced to be one of the Egyptian slaves building the pyramids.

As we finished each letter, and Peaches had the books neatly ordered back on the shelf, she sighed with satisfaction. `A place for everything, and everything in its place.´

Miss Wilkins breezed in now and again to check out how things were going. `Keep up the good work,´ she'd chirp, then breeze out again.

Zoot came into the library a lot, but just said, `Hi!´ and sat in the corner to read his big book about Australia. One time, Peaches asked him if he wanted to help us. Zoot smiled and said he was reading a really interesting part of his book and wanted to get to the end, so we left him alone. Bobby didn't though. He hunted Zoot down every day and dragged him out into the playground.

'What are you wasting your time in here for?' he said after lunch on Friday, grinning at me and Peaches as we worked on the M pile of books. 'This place is Yawn Central.'

Zoot slammed his book shut as his cousin leaned over to see what he was reading.

'I've got some Year Twos outside,' continued Bobby. 'I said I'd get you to sign autographs for them.'

Three excited faces peered through the window in the door, and Bobby beckoned the kids into the library.

'Can we have your autograph?' said the first one in, shoving a tatty piece of paper at Zoot. 'You're famous.'

'No I'm not,' he replied, glaring at his cousin. 'I'm not signing anything – sorry.'

The three kids looked confused and disappointed. 'You said he'd give us his autograph,' said the smallest one, scowling at Bobby. 'You said you were his boss.'

Bobby laughed nervously, and began shoving them back towards the door. 'Er, well I'm kind of looking after him,' he answered.

39

'You can have *my* autograph, if you like,' he said, pulling the newspaper clipping from his pocket and showing the young kids. 'I'm a famous runner.'

The kids looked impressed and seemed happy to let him scrawl his name on their scraps of paper. 'Those'll be worth a fortune when I win a gold medal at the Olympics,' he shouted as they left the library.

'My boss?' said Zoot.

Bobby laughed. 'I was joking! Listen, can you get George Looney to sign a few pieces of paper?' he said. 'Everyone wants his signature, and I said we could get some.'

'No way,' said Zoot.

'Oh, come on,' argued Bobby. 'It's only a few autographs . . .'

'No way,' repeated Zoot, more firmly.

'OK, OK,' said Bobby, raising his hands. He looked over at me and Peaches. 'Dump that book, and come and have a kick-around in the playground. If you stay in here too long you'll end up **Dull And Boring** like everyone else in here.'

Zoot frowned at his cousin. He sighed, pushed his big Australia book into his rucksack and headed out of the library. As Bobby followed him, he nudged the column of books by authors with names beginning with M, then scuttled out of the door. The tall stack wobbled and swayed.

'No!' cried Peaches as the pile of books tipped over.

I dashed forward and grabbed for the crumbling tower, but it toppled into the N pile, which crumpled over into the O pile, which smashed into the P pile. One by one, the stacks crashed down until all our carefully arranged books were spread across the floor.

'We'll just have to start again,' said Peaches. 'At least we'd already shelved letters A to L!'

On a scale of boring-osity, where 1 is

watching Algy play chess against his computer, and 100 is watching Emma and Gemma do ballet (which I have to do a lot of the time), then putting books in alphabetical order would have scored about 15,894,132,947. Doing it *twice* scored . . . whatever *twice* that number is.

Actually, it didn't take too long to do it this time. We carried on through afternoon break.

By the time Constanza arrived nine minutes late to take me home, Peaches and I had got all the stacks back in order and the books in the M, N, O and P piles on the bookshelves.

`So sorry I am late again, Ollie,´ Constanza said as she bustled into school. `I watch the soups.´

`Soaps,´ I corrected her.

`They are so exciting – BLAH-BLAH, BOOM-BOOM, BANG-BANG!´

She and Miss Wilkins had one of their whispered conversations. I heard words like `celebrity' . . . `newspaper' . . . `film stars' . . . and `dollop'.

`Ollie, why you no say to us about your new friend?' said Constanza as I climbed into the car. `He's a famous.'

`Zoot's not famous – his dad is,' I replied. `And he's not my friend.'

`Who's Zoot?' asked Emma.

`Who's his dad?' asked Gemma, both suddenly interested.

`Antonio Zipparolli,' I answered. `He's making a movie in town.'

Constanza turned to my sisters. `I find out George Looney is in the town also,' she told them.

'*What?*' yelled Emma and Gemma together, looking at me fiercely. 'Did you know?'

'Yes.'

The twins began to bash me with their ballet pumps. 'Why didn't you tell us?'

'I didn't think you'd be interested,' I said, trying to defend myself from the battering I was taking.

They stared wide-eyed and open-mouthed at me.

'Has your pea-brain stopped working completely?' wondered Emma, shaking her head in disbelief.

'You know someone who knows someone who knows George Looney,' spluttered Gemma. 'OF COURSE WE'RE INTERESTED!'

'Who's George Looney?' asked Algy. 'Does he play chess?'

I shrugged. 'He's a film star.'

Constanza sighed. 'He is *bellisimo*.'

The twins were furious that I'd kept them in the dark about George Looney, and didn't speak to me all weekend: result!

In fact, I was pretty much left alone by everyone. Mum was busy mending brains, Dad was away at a building-designing conference, Constanza was studying for her English exam and the twins were learning a new dance. Algy's exams were over, so he shut himself away in the basement, tinkering with the Zybot. He said I was lucky the toy hadn't blown up completely because my wires were crossed, my grommets were loose and my gaskets were leaky.

`Sorry, Ollie,´ he said, `but you're definitely not a **BRILLIANT** mechanical engineer.´

I trudged miserably back to my room and decided to do what I definitely *was* **BRILLIANT** at: reading **Agent Q** comics. I set out on a mammoth quest to reread every issue from 1 to 433

(not counting *Agent Q and the Doomsday Scrolls*, which was the only one I hadn't got).
I settled down to a spectacular weekend of adventure and strawberry milkshakes.

On Sunday evening, there was a knock at my bedroom door just as I'd started *Agent Q and the Invasion of the Donkey Snatchers*.

The Zybot stood outside, his red eyes glowing in the dark hallway. With a whirring sound, the toy raised its right hand, and said in a harsh, metallic voice, `Give . . . me . . . five . . . dude.´

It began to break-dance, swivelling its body, turning jerky somersaults and walking backwards, the eyes flashing in a silent disco beat. The **robot** did a final backflip, struck a cool pose and cried, 'Wicked . . . dude!'

'Awesome,' I breathed.

'I made a few improvements,' said my little brother, peeking round his bedroom door.

'How did you fix it?'

Algy took the back off the **robot**, and pointed out the nuts I hadn't tightened, and the places I'd got my wires crossed. 'Mending it wasn't as hard as I thought,' he said. 'But I decided to improve the voice box, so he'd say more, and upgrade the pumps so he'd move better.'

'I wish I was like you, Algy. I wish I was **BRILLIANT**, then Mum and Dad would leave me alone and stop pushing me all the time.'

'No they wouldn't,' he replied miserably. 'They don't leave *me* alone. They never stop pushing *me*.'

We both sighed, and stared silently at the Zybot, lost in our own thoughts. After a few moments, Algy said quietly, 'I'm sorry, Ollie. I only wanted to fix the **robot** so you could take it to school tomorrow for your **SHOW AND TELL**.'

I went cold. I'd forgotten all about PAIN AND TORTURE time.

'Thanks, Algy,' I said, taking the remote control from him. 'But it'd be cheating – you're the one who's made it work.'

I pressed a couple of buttons on the remote. The Zybot jerked as though it had been electrocuted, cried, 'Would . . . you . . . like . . . a . . . cup . . . of . . . tea?' then fell flat on its face.

'Besides,' I sighed, 'with my luck, it'd say a rude word to Miss Wilkins then destroy the classroom. Everyone would laugh and I'd get detention.'

'Well, what are you going to do then?' asked Algy, putting the toy back on its feet.

'I don't know. Constanza burned my toast this morning, and the scorch mark looks a bit like a kangaroo,' I told him.  'I kept it. Maybe I could show that.'

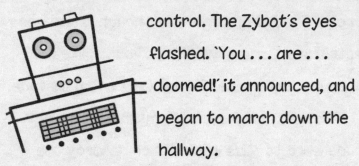

Algy pressed more buttons on the remote control. The Zybot's eyes flashed. `You . . . are . . . doomed!´ it announced, and began to march down the hallway.

`Good luck with that,´ said Algy, a Dr Devious grin spreading across his face. `I'm off to terrorize the twins.

CHAPTER 4

ATTACK OF THE MEGABOT!

The next morning, I sat in class with the piece of burnt toast in my bag, and listened to some great **SHOW AND TELL**s. Even the **DAB KIDS** had done something good.

Bobby Bragg had won his race and been selected to run for the county in the Regional Championships.

Millie Dangerfield told us she'd met her favourite writer, Jocelyn Wilton, and showed us her new book, *NIGHT OF THE VAMPIRE POODLES,* that had been signed by the author.

Hattie Hurley had done another word-search, with silly words like 'flibbertigibbet', 'whippersnapper' and 'kerfuffle'.

Peaches said she'd been to the National Bottle-top Museum, and showed us a badge she'd made from a lemon-pop bottle top in the museum's activity centre.

Jamie Ryder had got a new skateboard for his birthday.

Toby Hadron said he'd made a lie detector. He asked for a volunteer to demonstrate it, and I don't know why but everyone looked at me.

'Go on, Ollie,' called Jamie. 'Give us one of your big fat *FIBS.'*

I looked nervously towards Miss Wilkins.

`Go on then, Oliver,´ she smiled. `In the interests of science.´

I sat in a chair at the front of the class, while Toby stuck wires on my ears, nose and big toe. The wires curled into a machine that had dials and switches, and two light bulbs on the top.

`When you lie, your heart beats faster, you sweat a bit more and you blush,´ explained Toby. `The machine picks this up. If you tell the truth, the green light comes on, and the machine goes PING! If you tell a lie, the red

57

light flashes and the machine goes PONG!'

'Then get ready for a massive pong when Fibbs starts talking!' laughed Bobby Bragg.

'Right, let's get started,' said Toby. 'What's your name?'

'Oliver Fibbs.'

PONG! The red light flashed.

'I mean, Oliver *Tibbs*.'

PING! Now the green light came on.

'How extraordinary!' said Miss Wilkins. 'It works!'

'What did you do at the weekend, Oliver?' asked Toby.

I thought about how Bobby had been using Zoot to make himself look better . . . and then I thought . . . maybe I could use the Zybot for something after all.

WHAT IF...

'This weekend, I discovered that **DABMAN**'s arch-enemy, the Show-off was building a super-**robot**...' I said.

'The Show-off is planning to use the terrifying Megabot to destroy the DEFENDERS OF PLANET EARTH SECURITY and rule the world!'

PING!

Peaches smiled. `He's telling the truth!' she said.

Millie Dangerfield made a sound like a terrified sparrow. `Oh help! Who's going to save us?'

`Don't worry, Millie,' I said.

`This is a job for . . .

DABMAN!'

PING!

Toby frowned and flicked a few switches. `The lie detector seems to be broken.'

`It's M-A-L-F-U-N-C-T-I-O-N-I-N-G,' spelt out Hattie Hurley.

`Mal-what?' asked Bobby.

'I tested it this morning,' said Toby, thumping the metal box with his fist. 'There was nothing wrong.'

I went on with my story as he fiddled with the switches.

'The Megabot began its attack . . .'

PING!

Toby began to poke around inside the lie detector. 'This is most odd . . .'

I remembered the time in the library when Bobby knocked over our carefully stacked columns of books. **WHAT IF...**

`Oh no!' squeaked Millie. `Are **DABMAN** and Captain Common Sense OK?'

`Don't worry, Millie,' I replied. `They're alive and well.'

PING!

`The cockpit of my rocket ship has a special blast-proof capsule around it. The D.O.P.E.S. have been defeated for now, but we'll be back!'

PING!

Toby stared at the lie detector and scratched his head. `It's working properly,' he said, frowning. `Oliver seems to be telling the truth!'

`Wrong! Wrong! It should have gone PONG!' shouted Bobby Bragg.

`How extraordinary!' exclaimed Miss Wilkins. `Well, Oliver, we'll count that story as your

SHOW AND TELL, so you can go and sit down.'

I'd got away with it: the burnt toast stayed in my bag!

I pulled the sticky blobs that connected me to Toby's machine from my ears, nose and big toe, and hopped back to my seat to put my sock and shoe back on.

The rest of the class did their **SHOW AND TELL**s, until at last Zoot stood up.

'What did you do at the weekend, Zoot?' asked our teacher.

'My dad gave me a couple of lines to say in his movie,' he replied.

The whole class went, 'W o w w w w !'

'How dramatic!' said Miss Wilkins.

Zoot shrugged. 'It's no big deal.'

I leaned over towards Peaches. `This guy is cooler than the Head Cool Dude at the Cooldude Academy for Cool Dudes in Cooldude County, USA,´ I whispered.

Melody Nightingale was nearly jumping out of her chair with **excitement**. `What was your first line?´

`"**QUACK**",´ mumbled Zoot.

A few of the class tittered, and Zoot went red.

`I was dressed as a duck,´ he explained. `I was playing the part of a boy who tries to sell an Easter egg to George Looney as he chases a spy through a shopping mall.´

He showed us a photo of him and the great film star acting together. Zoot had a big yellow duck costume on, and you could just see his face peeking out through the beak.

'What was your other line?' asked Jamie Ryder.

'"**QUACK-QUACK**".'

This time the giggling was louder, and Zoot hurried back to his seat.

'How... **QUACKING**!' said Miss Wilkins.

At break, Peaches and I headed for the library to carry on the monster job of getting the books in order again. Zoot followed us in.

'Hey, Oliver, I liked your crazy story this morning,' he said. 'I just don't get what it had to do with **SHOW AND TELL**. Bobby says you do it all the time.'

I could feel my face getting hot. 'I never have anything interesting to **SHOW AND TELL**,' I mumbled. 'If I was **BRILLIANT** like the rest of my family it'd be OK, but I'm not, so I tell *FIBS*... I mean stories. Miss Wilkins used to give me playtime detentions and take away my SHINE TIME points, but as long as I write them down she doesn't seem to mind as much any more.'

Peaches smiled at Zoot. 'I liked yours,' she said. 'I've never met anyone who's been in a film before.'

Zoot shoved his hands deep in his pockets and stared at his feet. 'For the rest of my life I'll be known as the kid who played

67

the duck in that Zipparolli movie.´

'You might get a bigger part next time, as a secret agent, or a time-travelling treasure hunter, or something,´ I said.

'I don't want to be a film star,´ Zoot replied quietly. 'I just want . . .´

He did a cool, 'it's no big deal´ shrug of his shoulders, and headed for the chair in the corner to read his big book about Australia.

CHAPTER 5

SURPRISE!

The bell rang for the end of break. As I rushed round the end of a row of shelves heading for the door, I collided into Zoot just as he was on his way out. The massive book on Australia tumbled from his hands and clattered to the floor.

I began to apologize, but stopped as I bent down to pick up the book. I couldn't believe my eyes. A comic hidden inside the pages had fallen out too. It was a copy of *Agent Q and the CARROT OF CERTAIN DEATH*.

Zoot's face flushed as red as the bloodthirsty mutant carrot in the story. He grabbed the comic and shoved it back among the pages of the book.

`I . . . I don't know what that's doing in there,´ he stammered. `I, er . . . I found it when I opened the book.´

`*Agent Q and the CARROT OF CERTAIN DEATH* is one of my favourites,´ I said. `I love the bit when **Q** is pushed off the top of a cliff by the killer carrot, and uses his hair as a parachute to stop him going *splat* on the bottom.'

Zoot's eyebrows shot upwards, and his mouth dropped open like a big letter O. 'You like reading **Agent Q** comics?'

Here we go, I thought. I know what's coming next. 'Nobody reads those stupid comics any more. Bobby was right about you: you're **Dull And Boring**.'

But he didn't say that. Zoot glanced around to see if anyone was listening, then whispered, 'I love **Agent Q**! He's *soooooo* cool! My favourite part is in **Agent Q and the** PIRATES OF PIRANHA BAY, when he has to walk the plank over man-eating fish-infested waters, but he escapes by bouncing off the end and . . .'

`. . . his special-agent raincoat turns into a hang-glider,´ I said, `propellers shoot out from the buttons and he flies away across the sea!´ I suddenly realized why he'd been spending so much time in the library. `You've not been reading about Australia: you've been hiding your comics in a big book, like I do!´

`I've never met anyone else who likes **Agent Q** comics,´ said Zoot.

`Well, you have now!´ laughed Peaches. `Ollie's got hundreds of them.´

`Why don't you come round to my house after school?´ I suggested. `We can read some of them, and you can stay for dinner. Our nanny Constanza's making Italian meatballs.´

`*Fantastico!*´ he cried. `I'll phone my dad and tell him.´

Constanza was fifteen minutes late picking us up at the end of school, so Zoot and I went to help Peaches finish organizing all the books into alphabetical order.

'I've nearly done it,' she said. 'This is the V pile, and that's the W pile, and there are no authors with names beginning with X, so that lonely one's the Z pile.' She pointed to a single book lying on the floor nearby. 'It's by Zelda Zipparolli.' Peaches gasped. 'Oh! That's your name!'

'That's my mom,' he explained. 'She writes children's books.'

I went to pick it up, but Peaches stopped me, and began shoving me and Zoot into the corridor.

'I can manage on my own now. See you

75

tomorrow,' she said, closing the door.

'She's **awesome**,' said Zoot. 'Is she always so . . .'

'Bossy?'

'Sensible.'

'Always.'

Constanza hurried into school. 'So sorry, Oliver!' she said. 'I take the twins to the doctor. They have an itchy all over! It's a *mystero*!'

Zoot and I flicked through the pages of the comic while she and Miss Wilkins gossiped for a while. As usual, I caught the odd word: '**robot**', 'celebrity', 'cute' and 'pig farm'.

When they were finished, I introduced Zoot to Constanza, and he spoke to her in Italian. (Honestly, he was so cool he could grow icicles.)

We climbed into the back seat of the car

next to Algy, who had a
Dr Devious grin on his
face again.

`Did you hear about the
twins?´ he said with a wink.
`What could have given them
the itchy-snitchies?´

`Maybe it was something they ate,´ I
suggested.

`Or maybe the Zybot went into their room
and put itching
powder in their
leotards,´ he
whispered
with a
dastardly
grin.

THE WORLD'S ICHIEST ITCHING POWDER

I told Zoot that Algy was a chess champion, and it turned out that Zoot had won the California Junior Chess League two years before. `Maybe we can have a game sometime?´ he suggested.

`Yes, please!´ beamed my little brother. `It'll make a change from playing on my computer.´

Zoot gasped when we got into my room at home and he saw the collection of **Agent Q** comics. `You've even got the first issue: **Agent Q and the** BIG STINK! I've never seen that one!´

`If I ever find a copy of **Agent Q and the Doomsday Scrolls**, I'll have the full set,´ I replied. `But it's incredibly rare.´

`I've got one at home in the States!´ said Zoot.

My mouth dropped open. I tried to speak, but all that came out was a squeaky choking sound.

Zoot laughed. `Hey, why don't I get my dad's secretary to fly my copy over so you can read it?´

I made spitty, coughing noises this time, but then managed to say, `That'd be *spectacular*.´

There was a knock on my door and the twins swept into the room, beaming sweet, sickly smiles.

`Hi, Ollie-kins,´ said Emma, her voice oozing like sticky syrup.

`Can we come in, Ollie-pops?´ trilled Gemma, sounding like a canary.

`I smell a rat,´ I whispered to Zoot. `Just like in **Agent Q and the Double Agent Double Deal**, when **Q** is offered a truce by his arch-rival Z.´

'Would you and your new friend like to
join us for refreshments in the sitting room?'
suggested Emma, talking as though she had a
mouthful of plums.

'Tea? Cupcakes? Macaroons?' asked
Gemma, sounding like a princess, but scratching
her sides like a monkey. (Algy's itching powder
had *really* done the trick.)

'I remember what happens' said Zoot. 'Z
hands **Agent Q** a bag containing half a million

dollars in exchange for his sunglasses . . .'

`And when **Agent Q** opens the bag . . .'

'We just wanted to make your new friend feel welcome in our home,' said Emma and Gemma together.

'No thanks,' I said, pushing them back towards the door. 'We're going to read **𝘈𝘨𝘦𝘯𝘵 𝘘** comics until dinnertime.'

'Ollie-kins said you know George Looney,' continued Emma, scratching her tummy and batting her eyes at Zoot.

'Is it true what everyone's saying?' asked Gemma. 'Is he going out with Ritzy Savoy?'

I gave them another shove to get them out into the hallway. As I closed the door, the twins continued to smile, scratch and wave.

`Catch you later, Zoot!´

`Ciao!´

A shudder rattled through my body. `Creepy. I prefer them when they're threatening to chop me into pieces and feed me to chickens.´

Zoot sighed. `It always happens,´ he said quietly, tracing his finger along the top of my desk. `As soon as people find out who my dad is, they're incredibly nice to me. But they're not interested in *me*, only whose autograph I can get for them . . .´

He pulled a comic from the shelf. `Hey, do you wanna come over to my house for dinner sometime?´ He dropped his voice. `George Looney and Ritzy Savoy are there most nights.´

`Ritzy Savoy? You never said she was in the film.´

'Shh! Keep your voice down!' whispered Zoot. 'She's *not* in the film, but she *is* George's girlfriend. It's top secret. They don't want the gossip magazines to find out for sure, or they'll be pestered by photographers and it'll spoil the filming. So, do you wanna come round?'

'That'd be great,' I answered. 'But don't tell the twins, or they'll flatten me flatter than **Agent Q** was flattened by Moola the Crazy Cash Cow.'

`Yeah,´ laughed Zoot, `and you've not got
Q's secret-agent re-inflation device inserted in
your belly button!´

CHAPTER 6

TRAITOR!

The next morning, Zoot strolled into the classroom and sat down next to me and Peaches.

`I asked Miss Wilkins if I could sit with you in class from now on,´ he explained. `Is that OK with you guys?´

`Yeah, course it is,´ I replied, glancing at Bobby. It was a good thing he didn´t have laser eyes like Algy´s Zybot, or the three of us would have been frazzled on the spot.

'You know that if you always sit with us, you're officially **Dull And Boring**?' Peaches warned him.

Zoot smiled and gave a cool, 'do I look like I care?' kind of shrug.

I opened my bag and showed him the huge book that my mum and dad had bought me: *The Age of the Machine – Robots and Artificial Intelligence for Beginners.*

'There's a copy of **Agent Q and the SUPERSONIC STICK-UP** hidden inside,' I whispered. 'We can start reading it in the library at break.'

'As long as you both keep out of my way,' said Peaches. 'I've finished sorting out the fiction books, and I've started the non-fiction.'

Bobby's laser eyes were fixed on Zoot all

morning, but Zoot took no notice. When the bell rang for breaktime, Zoot and I hurried to the library to read my comic. As we settled into the bean-bags in Peaches' new Bookworm Corner, I glanced up and noticed Bobby frowning at us through the window.

'He's giving you evils again,' I muttered. Zoot just shook his head, and carried on reading.

We were totally engrossed as **Agent Q** had discovered the hideout of Sangster the Gangster and the High B-flats, her troupe of bank-robbing opera singers. The villainous vocalist crept up on our hero . . .

'Caught you red-handed!' said a voice behind us, which was spooky, as that's exactly what Sangster the Gangster said to **Agent Q.**

Bobby Bragg reached over and snatched the comic, holding it as though it was laced with poison. 'I warned you, Zoot,' he said. 'Anyone who hangs around Fibbs too long catches his Boring Bug — looks like it's already got you.'

'Ollie's cool,' replied Zoot.

I was as shocked as Bobby. 'Am I?'

'Yes, you are,' said Peaches, who had hurried over to see what was going on.

Zoot took the comic from Bobby and handed it to me. 'Ollie's not boring — he's funny, and friendly, and he likes stories. You know, cuz, just because you win medals, or swim fast, or score lots of soccer goals, doesn't make you better than everyone else.'

Bobby's face twisted and scrunched in a mixture of anger and disbelief. 'But . . . but . . . you're supposed to be on *my* side,' he stammered.

'I'm on no one's side,' answered Zoot. 'Ollie's my pal, so I'm going to hang out with him and read comics.'

'Be a loser then,' said Bobby, leaning close to Zoot. 'Traitor,' he growled, and stormed out of the library.

'Uh-oh, looks like you're banned from the Super And Special table at lunchtime,' I said.

Zoot shrugged. 'So, are you guys gonna to come to my house tomorrow night?' He glanced around the library. 'George and Ritzy are gonna be there,' he whispered.

Peaches frowned. 'Well, I was going to stay behind after school and adjust the settings on the new copier in the library. It says in the instructions that if you're careful you can make perfect copies . . .'

My jaw dropped.

'Duh!' she laughed. 'I'd love to come.'

At home, I tried to be cool about the invitation, but my parents were thrilled: at last I was doing something interesting.

'Tell Mr Zipparolli that you got a Bronze

Star in your Grade Two Speaking Poetry Aloud exam,' suggested Dad. `He might cast you in his next film.'

`All those acting lessons we paid for last year might pay off yet,' added Mum.

> To pee or not to pee, that is the question

I decided not to mention that I'd be meeting George Looney and Ritzy Savoy. I didn't know if my family would be able to cope with the excitement, and I didn't know if I could cope with the twins pestering me to get autographs or film-star gossip. But just as I was getting out of the car to go into school the next morning I couldn't resist dropping my celebrity-bomb on the twins. They were in mid-ballet-babble.

`Madame Picamole says my *allongé* is far more elegant than Crystal Fortesque-Smyth's,' said Emma.

`I'm not surprised. Crystal's *ballon* is as bouncy as a burst balloon,' added Gemma.

`And as for Tanya Kaminsky . . .'

`I'll say "hi" to George Looney for you, shall I?' I said casually as I slid from the car.

`What?' they replied together.

'I'm meeting him tonight at Zoot's house. Didn't I tell you?'

The twins couldn't have been more shocked than if I'd slapped them both in the face with a wet kipper.

'*Ciao!*' I called cheerily, slamming the car door and setting off down the path to school.

I turned to give them a wave, and couldn't help grinning at the look of fury on their faces. Their mouths opened and closed comically as they screamed and wailed at me from inside the car. Algy laughed and covered his ears. Gemma's window rolled down as Constanza drove away from school, and the words 'worm', 'slimeball' and 'toad' fizzed through the air like bullets.

Peaches skipped over to me. As usual, she

had her `sensible satchel´ slung over one shoulder, with all the things she might need to get her through the day. This morning, she had so much packed inside that the bag was bulging to bursting point.

`What've you got in there?´ I asked.

`Nosy crows will lose their nose,´ she replied. `Wait and see.´

Our good mood didn't last long.

`Hey, guys,´ said Zoot as we went into the classroom together. `I thought I'd better tell you that Bobby's gonna be at my house tonight too. My dad's invited the whole family over and Bobby *is* my cousin, after all.´

My heart dropped like the broken lift in **Agent Q and the HELLHOLE HOTEL.**

*

Bobby ignored Zoot all day. At lunchtime, I saw him point at the three of us and say something to Toby and Hattie. They laughed, and Bobby's lip curled into a sneer. It was going to be a *fun* evening.

At the end of the day, Mr Zipparolli's gleaming white stretch limo purred to a halt outside school. Kids and parents crowded round, peering through the black-tinted windows, and taking photos with their phones.

'Where's Pea?' I wondered, searching among the people swarming about on the pavement.

'There,' answered Zoot, pointing to a girl walking towards us.

I didn't recognize my best friend. She had brushed her hair out of the two bunches she

normally wore, and changed into her best blue dress, with silver pumps on her feet, and a small, shiny silver bag hung over one shoulder. Long, glittery butterfly earrings fluttered from her ears, to match the butterfly necklace round her neck.

'Pea?'

Peaches smiled. 'I'm meeting film stars,' she said. 'I need to sparkle. These shoes aren't very sensible though – I'm going to have blisters the size of boiled eggs tomorrow.'

'You look . . . neat,' said Zoot, his face going red.

`Thank you,´ replied Peaches, blushing too.
`I've brought your mum's book,´ she continued
quickly. `Do you think she'd sign it for the school?´

`Mum'd sign a bus ticket,´ joked Zoot.

The driver opened the back door of the limo,
and we stepped into a glittering magical cave. A
white leather sofa ran down one side of the car,
and curved round the back. On the opposite side
were gleaming cabinets. The roof was lit up with
swirling waves of blue neon lights, while the floor
was made of thick, clear plastic and had tropical
fish swimming under our feet!

`It's playtime, guys,´ said Zoot. `Watch
this.´ He picked up a remote control and pressed
a button. A TV screen swung down from the
ceiling. `It's got satellite-TV, Game-World Seven,
all my dad's movies . . .´

A green light flashed on the wall nearby, and made a *peep-peep* sound.

Zoot pushed it, and said, 'Hi, James.'

The driver's voice came from a speaker in the roof of the car. 'Please fasten your seatbelts,' he said. 'As you can see from the satellite navigation screen at the front of your cabin, our estimated journey time today will be thirty-two minutes. The cabin temperature is set at twenty degrees. Please adjust for your own comfort, and enjoy the journey.'

As the car set off, Zoot opened a fridge door. 'We've got ice cream, cold drinks or I can microwave a fruit pie . . .'

I flicked a switch on the table next to me, and the door of one of the cabinets slid back with a soft whirring sound. There was some kind of drinks dispenser inside.

Zoot grinned at me. 'And *that* is the coolest gadget of them all,' he said. 'It's a machine that makes strawberry milkshakes.'

I was speechless. This car was like something out of an **Agent Q** comic.

We spent the whole thirty-two minutes to Zoot's house pressing buttons, drinking milkshakes and playing Draco the Droid Destroyer on the Game-World Seven.

If Bobby didn't spoil it, maybe it wasn't going to be such a bad night after all!

CHAPTER 7

STARS IN THEIR EYES!

The limo pulled up outside Mr Zipparolli's mansion, and James helped Peaches as she stepped from the car. Zoot's mum and dad came down the steps to greet us. Zoot had just introduced us when we heard a squeal of brakes and the growl of a high-powered engine. A gleaming silver Ferroni sports car sped up the driveway towards us.

Zoot's dad laughed and shook his head.

`Here come the Braggs.´

Bobby's dad was driving, and with screeching, smoking tyres, he threw the car into a handbrake turn then reversed at speed the final twenty metres to the front of the house. I saw Bobby grinning at us from the back seat as his dad revved the engine hard before finally turning it off.

`New motor, Antonio,´ shouted Mr Bragg, leaping from the car. `Top of the range, nought to sixty in three nanoseconds, and cost me over a hundred grand. Better than that walloping great bus of a limo you've got!'

'It's very nice, Robert,' said Mr Zipparolli.
'But a little too noisy for me.'

'Hey, Junior, get out of the car,' yelled
Bobby's dad. 'Your mates are here.'

Bobby strolled over to us, and nodded at
the Ferroni. 'Cool set of wheels, eh, Zoot?'

Zoot shrugged.

'I like the colour,' said Peaches. 'It won't
show the dirt.'

'Sis!' called out Bobby's mum, kissing
Mrs Zipparolli on each cheek. 'Loved your new
book, *The Howl Factor*! TV talent show and
werewolves – great stuff.'

'I found one of your other books in the
school library,' said Peaches, pulling a pen from
her little silver bag. 'Would you sign it, please?'

'Come into the house and meet the stars,' said Zoot's mum, scribbling her name on the title page.

We left Bobby and his dad giving Mr Zipparolli a tour of the new car, and went inside.

'I didn't know you were in the film,' said Peaches when she met Ritzy Savoy.

The two famous actors glanced at each other and smiled.

'I'm not,' Ritzy answered. 'I've come to see George. I love your earrings.'

Bobby's mum pushed in front of Peaches. 'And I love

your diamond ring!' she said to Ritzy, grasping the film star's left hand. 'It's just like the one Bobby Senior bought me when we got engaged, only my diamond's bigger.' She waggled her hand to show off the sparkly jewel on her finger. 'How much did it cost?'

'I don't know. You'd better ask George,' replied Ritzy.

Mrs Bragg hurried over to talk to George Looney, who was chatting with Zoot's mum.

Peaches stared at the ring on Ritzy's finger. 'Are you and Mr Looney *really* getting married?'

Ritzy smiled, and put her finger to her lips. 'It's a secret. We're going to announce it when the filming's finished. We'll have photographers and reporters pestering us day and night when they find out, and George doesn't want the film to be spoiled.'

Zoot took the three of us up to his room before dinner. It was huge, and had a pool table, a TV, a bookcase full of books and comics, a computer and . . . a Zybot!

`I thought it was cool that you were building a **robot,** so I thought I'd have a go too,' said Zoot. `But I can't get it to work – I'm useless at stuff like that.'

`Just like you, Fibbs,' said Bobby, opening a game on Zoot's computer.

Zoot ignored him. `I was gonna ask if you could try to fix it for me.'

I took the back off the Zybot and peered inside. I remembered how Algy said he'd repaired mine, and after checking the instruction manual

I began to move some wires around, and fiddle
with the pumps. I ummed and ahhed, nodded
intelligently and repeated some of the words
Algy had used, like `sprocket´, `gasket´ and
`flange´. I reconnected the batteries, and got
ready to turn on the toy.

 `Have you got a water pistol handy, by any
chance?´ I asked Zoot.

 `No, why?´ he asked.

 `Never mind.´ I held my breath and pressed
the green `POWER´ button on the remote
control.

 The Zybot whirred into life. I shoved the
joystick forward and it
strode towards Zoot,
growling, `He-llo,
Mas-ter!´

Zoot and Peaches were *totally* amazed, but not as amazed as I was. You could have felled me with a fig-roll.

`Thanks, Ollie,´ said Zoot. `You're **BRILLIANT**!´

Bobby laughed scornfully behind me. I shrugged like I'd seen Zoot do, in a cool, `it was nothing´ kind of way. Luckily, Zoot's mum called us down to dinner before the **robot** had a chance to blow up and ruin everything.

Dinner was fantastic: the grown-ups had plate after plate of fiddly fancy food, but we had pizza with *any* topping we wanted!

`Of course, at home,´ said Mrs Bragg, `Bobby Junior often has caviar on his pizza.´

`Not *that* often, Mum,´ said Bobby, frowning at his mother, and fidgeting with his knife and fork.

Zoot leaned over and whispered to me, 'It's fish eggs! Bobby once told me he sneaks it to the dog under the table!'

Mrs Bragg laughed and pinched her son's cheek. 'Have I embarrassed you, Bobby-kin?'

'No,' said Bobby, pulling away from his mum. 'I'd like big chunks of steak on my pizza, please.'

'Good lad!' barked Mr Bragg. 'Food of champions. Will make you strong.'

I asked for pepperoni and baked beans, and when the pizza came I saw that the chef had made a pepperoni volcano in the centre, with a lava flow of beans cascading down the meaty mountain and spreading out across the cheese and tomato base. There was *no way* Mum would have let me get away with that – spectacular!

111

`Ever thought about going into business, George?' asked Mr Bragg, munching on a mouthful of smoked salmon.

The film star opened his mouth to answer, but Bobby Senior carried on regardless. `I export to twenty-three countries and I'm opening a factory in China next month. I come from a family of winners. When Bobby Junior takes over the family business, he'll be a winner too.'

`He's sprinting in the County Championship finals on Sunday,' said Mrs Bragg.

'And losing's not allowed,' added Mr Bragg, pointing his knife at his son.

'Don't worry, Dad,' said Bobby, glancing at Zoot. 'I'll win.'

'Pea won a Jolly Roger badge last month,' I told everyone. 'You know, from the TV programme. She collected plastic bottle tops to help save the South American warty toad from extinction.'

It was like **SHOW AND TELL**: all the grown-ups went, 'Oooooooooo.'

Peaches blushed. 'Ollie! George and Ritzy both won Oscars last year; they won't be impressed because I won a Jolly Roger badge.'

'Are you kidding?' exclaimed George. 'You helped save a toad! How cool is that!'

113

`I *always* wanted a Jolly Roger badge,´ said Ritzy. `But I never won one – I think I'd rather have that than an Oscar!´

After dinner, we all headed for the enormous games room. There was another pool table, a dartboard, table tennis and dozens of board games.

George and Ritzy were great fun. Peaches and I beat them at pool, but lost at Twister.

Later on, Zoot asked me to tell one of my **FIBS,** so I did the one about the GIANT BOY-MUNCHING BUGS. As I told the story, George and Ritzy acted out some of the scenes with me and Peaches, pretending to be man-eating plants and killer frogs.

Every time the Show-off was mentioned, I saw Peaches glance at Bobby Junior, but he just sat there, stony-faced and silent. He was like an overfilled balloon all evening, tight and ready to burst at the slightest jab. He didn't speak much, and made sure he wasn't against Zoot in any game we played.

As we were getting ready to leave, I asked Mr Looney if he would sign two autographs to Emma and Gemma.

'I'll give you my autograph, if you give me yours,' he replied.

'Why do you want mine?'

'Because I think you'll be famous one day.'

'Yeah, Oliver Tibbs and his Big Fat *FIBS!*' said Bobby.

George laughed. 'They're not *FIBS*, are

they Ollie?' he said. 'They're stories!'

I'd had the best night of my life, and was just thinking what a totally amazing **SHOW AND TELL** this was going to make on Monday, when Ritzy Savoy took us to one side.

'Kids, *please* don't tell anyone I was here,' she said. 'The press are sniffing around, and if it gets out that George and I are getting married we won't have a minute's peace. Do you promise to keep it a secret?'

'We promise.'

Bobby and his parents roared away with another squeal of tyres, and James took me and Peaches home in the limo.

When I walked into the house, my family were waiting for me in the hallway.

'Well? Did you meet George Looney?' asked Emma.

'Or was it one of your little jokes?' added Gemma.

'Yeah, he was there, and so was –' I froze, remembering my promise – 'Peaches.'

'Did you talk to him?' asked Mum.

'Yeah, and we played games with him and . . . Zoot's mum.'

It was a nightmare! They fired questions at me, and went 'ooo' and 'ahh' when I answered them, but I managed to get through my interrogation without mentioning Ritzy once. Finally, I gave my sisters their autographs.

`Ollie! You're the best brother ever!' screeched Emma. `Even if you are a worm!'

`And a slimeball,' squealed Gemma.

`And a toad,' they added together.

You see? They love me really.

CHAPTER 8

THE CHALLENGE

On Monday morning, Zoot reminded Peaches, Bobby and me that we were sworn to secrecy about George and Ritzy.

'I had a friend in the States who took sneaky photos with his phone on the set of one of my dad's films, and sold them to the press,' he told us. 'Dad went ballistic, and that kid's not my friend any more.'

'The sensible thing to do is not say anything

about it at all,´ suggested Peaches. `Just in case.´

`I don´t need to talk about the party,´ said Bobby. `I´ve always got something good to say for **SHOW AND TELL** – unlike some people.´

When Miss Wilkins called him up, he shot from his chair and strode to the front.

`On Sunday, I won the Regional one hundred metres race,´ he announced, holding up his gold medal. `I´ve qualified for the national squad trials. ´

`How fantastic!´ cried Miss Wilkins, leading the class in applause.

Bobby stared at Zoot, and didn't take his eyes off him all the way back to his seat. I saw him whisper something to Toby Hadron as he sat down again.

The other kids stood up and did their presentations.

Leon Curley had grown a lemon tree from a pip.

Millie Dangerfield had made a sock-puppet.

Toby Hadron said he'd made alterations to his lie detector – The Ping Pong Machine – and it was foolproof now.

He looked at me.

I looked at Miss Wilkins.

She looked amused.

There were more sticky blobs and wires than last time, but after lots of fiddling the

machine was finally ready. Toby asked me a few easy questions to test that the PINGs and PONGs were working properly. Then he asked me what we did at Zoot's house on Friday night.

I looked at Peaches and saw her mime a zip going across her mouth.

'We had pizza and played Twister,' I said.

PING!

'Who was there?' he asked.

As I went through the list, the machine went PING after each name. I didn't mention Ritzy.

Toby glanced at Bobby, who nodded. 'Is that everyone?'

'Yes,' I replied.

PONG!

'Lie! Lie! You're a pumpkin pie!' shouted
Bobby.

'Who else was there?' asked Toby.

Zoot flashed me a look of warning as Bobby
grinned triumphantly.

'Er . . . well . . . there was another person
there,' I said. 'James, the driver!'

PING!

Bobby looked furious, and opened his
mouth to say something else. He was obviously
trying to make me spill the beans about the
engagement, and make Zoot fall out with me. I
had to think of something quick.

I thought about how if I hadn't helped
Peaches organize the library, I wouldn't have

125

found out that Zoot liked **Agent Q** comics, and he wouldn't have become our friend.

WHAT IF...

`Something else happened this weekend,´ I told the class. `The Megabot had destroyed the D.O.P.E.S. headquarters, but Captain Common Sense and I managed to escape. We went undercover, and set up a new HQ inside a school library...

PING!

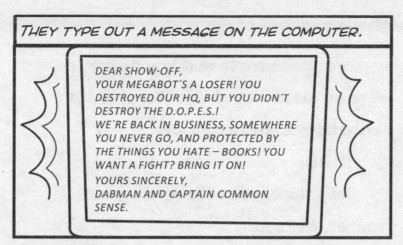

THEY TYPE OUT A MESSAGE ON THE COMPUTER.

DEAR SHOW-OFF,
YOUR MEGABOT'S A LOSER! YOU
DESTROYED OUR HQ, BUT YOU DIDN'T
DESTROY THE D.O.P.E.S.!
WE'RE BACK IN BUSINESS, SOMEWHERE
YOU NEVER GO, AND PROTECTED BY
THE THINGS YOU HATE – BOOKS! YOU
WANT A FIGHT? BRING IT ON!
YOURS SINCERELY,
DABMAN AND CAPTAIN COMMON
SENSE.

PING!

`You see,´ I heard Millie Dangerfield whisper

to Leon Curley. `It is true.´

`The **SAS GANG** got our message,´ I went on,

`and took the bait...´

WARTS! THEY'RE HIDING IN THE LIBRARY!

BOOKS DON'T INTIMIDATE ME!

YOUR BIG WORDS WILL BE NO USE – THE PLACE IS FULL OF DICTIONARIES!

SEND IN THE MEGABOT. I'VE INCREASED HIS POWER!

127

'We didn't have to wait long before we heard the *stomp, stomp, stomp,* of the **robot**'s massive metal boots.'

PING!

Toby stared at the lie detector and frowned. 'Not again . . .'

I looked around the classroom. Everyone was gripped by my story.

'The Megabot smashed through the doors, its laser eyes flashing. Captain Common Sense stepped out from behind the librarian's counter and began to read from a book.'

PING!

Toby had been checking his machine while I talked. He scratched his head. `I don't get it,´ he said. `The machine was working properly when we started.´

Bobby Bragg groaned in frustration. `It's broke! It's broke! The story is a joke!´

'While the android was distracted by the tale of Rosie the Robot's missing teddy,' I continued, 'I sneaked up behind and carefully unscrewed the control panel on its back.'

DABMAN MESSES WITH WIRES AND SWITCHES INSIDE THE ROBOT.

FIZZ! FLASH!

If this doesn't work, we're doomed!

HELLO, CAN I BE A D.O.P.E.?

WELCOME TO THE GANG!

Time for a raspberry ripple ice cream!

PING!

'I don't understand it, miss,' said Toby Hadron. 'Oliver is *definitely* telling the truth.'

Miss Wilkins smiled. 'Well, Oliver's stories are very real to him.'

'Or I really *am **DABMAN***!' I protested.

PING!

Bobby snorted. 'Well, ***DABMAN***,' he said, 'the Show-off's not going to give up that easily.'

Toby pulled the tangle of wires off me, and the other kids did their **SHOW AND TELL**s.

Hattie Hurley presented us with yet another Word Search, this time with rude words like, 'balderdash', 'baloney', and 'bunkum'.

Peaches told everyone that the library reorganization was finished, and showed us a plan of the shelves, explaining where each section was.

Finally, Zoot stood up. `I've not done anything special this week, just read a few **Agent Q** comics with Ollie.´

`How . . . literary!´ said Miss Wilkins. `I heard you're a really good runner. Why don't you tell the class about that?´

Zoot nodded. `Sure. Last year, I broke the North American Junior hundred metres record.´

Once again, the class went, `W o w w w w w !´

`How extraordinary!´ exclaimed Miss Wilkins.

`You'll be able to race against Bobby at the school Sports Day next week,´ said

Jamie Ryder, grinning at Bobby.

A murmur of excitement rippled through the class.

`Did *you* break any records this weekend, Bobby?´ asked Jamie.

`No,´ answered Bobby, his voice as sharp and cold as an icicle. `But I'm doing special training. I'm getting faster and faster.´

At break, Zoot's eyes lit up when I showed him the comic I'd brought in to read at lunchtime: **Agent Q and** *the Slippers of Shame.*

`That's the one with Grizzly Grandma and her ferocious false teeth! I can't wait! By the way,´ he went on, my copy of **Agent Q and the** *Doomsday Scrolls* is on the plane. We should have it by Friday.´

*

With each day that passed, I was getting more and more excited at the thought of finally reading the one comic I didn't have. Everyone else seemed just as excited about Sports Day. The sprinting contest between Bobby and Zoot was the talk of the school.

Every break and lunchtime, Bobby went on to the school field, practising his starts, and sprinting up and down. He would stop now and again to do press-ups and sit-ups then jumps to his feet and dash across the grass once more. He'd asked Toby Hadron to put together a scientifically proven training programme and special diet. (No pizza, I bet!)

Toby stood with a stopwatch, timing

Bobby's runs, counting his press-ups and writing things down on charts.

'He's really serious,' I said as we watched through the library window.

'He's really *worried*,' said Peaches. 'You saw what his parents are like. Bobby *has* to win.'

CHAPTER 9

THE DOOMSDAY SCROLLS

On Friday morning, Zoot was waiting for me at the school gates, and hurried over as I got out of the car. He was carrying a huge library book, *The Joy of Geology*, by Petronella Rocklady.

The twins glanced at him, then carried on talking about their dancing. They'd got their George Looney autograph, and so Zoot wasn't interesting to them any more.

'Ooo, rocks rock!' said Algy, reaching for the big book. 'Can I have a look?'

'Er, not just now, Algy,' replied Zoot. 'I'll bring it round to your house tonight when I come over to play chess with you.'

He cracked open the book a little to show me what was hidden inside. The cover of *Agent Q and the Doomsday Scrolls* peeked out from the pages.

I tried to speak, but nothing came out of my mouth. I'd dreamed of this moment: at last, I was finally going to read the only *Agent Q* story that I'd never read before.

138

`Wow,´ I breathed.

We took our places in class, and Zoot put the rock book in his tray under the desk. All morning, the comic seemed to be calling, `Ollie! Read me, read me!´ It was torture! I stared at the table top, wishing I had X-ray eyes to be able to see the story through the wood.

Just before break, Leon Curley had a nose-bleed trying to work out a really hard sum. Hattie Hurley took one look at the blood dripping from his nose and fainted.

As everyone fussed around them, I pulled open the drawer and sneaked a quick look at the comic. I noticed Bobby Bragg looking over to see what I was doing, so snapped the book closed and joined the rest of the class going `euugh!´ and `gross!´ at Leon.

At long last, the bell rang for break, and Zoot and I charged to the library and flopped down on the bean bags in Bookworm Corner. The story was fantastic. The *Doomsday Scrolls* contained an ancient spell that if said out loud would bring about the end of civilization. It had been lost for centuries. Everyone thought the world was safe, but the evil scientist Doctor Destructor had made a time machine and gone back to when the *Doomsday Scrolls* were written. He intended to steal them, bring them back to the present and hold the world to ransom.

Agent Q had stowed away on the time machine . . .

I could hardly breathe. How was going to escape this time? As the bony, rotting hands of King Tootonmahorn tightened round Q's neck, Zoot turned the page . . .

Just then I heard Peaches' voice shout, 'Look out! Danger!'

'I know!' I replied. ''s doomed!'

A hand reached between us and snatched the comic out of the big book.

Zoot leaped to his feet. 'Give it back, Bobby!'

Bobby sneered and waved the comic in Zoot's face.

'Be careful,' I said. 'That's a really rare edition.'

The fire alarm began to wail loudly like a cow with toothache. As we all covered our ears,

I glanced behind Bobby and saw
thick green smoke drifting
past the window.

Our head teacher, Mrs
Broadside, burst through the library door. `Drop
everything and get out into the playground!' she
shouted.

Bobby hurled **Agent Q and the
Doomsday Scrolls** over his shoulder, barged
past Peaches and sprinted for the door. Zoot
scrambled over the bean bags to reach his
comic.

`Leave it, Zoot!' yelled Mrs Broadside. `This
is an emergency! Get out NOW!'

She pushed and hurried the three of us
out of the library, slamming the door shut
behind her. A stinky, pea-coloured smog swirled

around the corridor and hung in the classrooms. We dashed, coughing and spluttering, into the playground.

'What's happened?' I asked Jamie Ryder.

He grinned. 'Toby Hadron's Primordial Soup exploded in his bag!'

Two firemen in breathing gear went into the school, and a moment later came out carrying Toby's smoking bag. They doused it with foam, then handed it back to him.

'My experiment's ruined!' moaned Toby, peering at the drippy, gooey mess sloshing around inside the bag.

I saw the picture in my mind. '**WHAT IF . . .** the foam is the vital ingredient you needed to create new life?' I said. '**WHAT IF . . .** tonight, while you're asleep, a foam monster grows from the liquid and comes after you, its ~~slimy green~~ hands reaching out for your throat? **WHAT IF . . .'**

   'That'll do, Oliver,' said Miss Wilkins, looking at Toby's worried face. 'The firemen have opened all the windows and doors, and say it's safe to go back into school.'

   'What about **Agent Q and the Doomsday Scrolls?'** said Zoot. 'It's lying on the floor of the library. I need to get it.'

   'Don't worry,' said Peaches. 'I've got permission to spend the rest of the morning in the library to get it ready for the official opening next week. I'm leaving school before lunchtime, so I'll put your comic in a safe place before I go.´

`Where are you going?´ I asked.

`I'm counting sheep on the Porkney Isles with my mum and dad. We're taking part in the National Sheep Survey. It'll be interesting. No phone signal, no internet, no telly . . .´

`No pizza,´ I added.

`Well, at least you'll get some sleep,´ said Zoot. `You know, counting all those sheep.´

Peaches laughed. `I'll put the comic inside a big book called, *The Lives of British Prime Ministers*. It's by the Right Honourable David Cameroon, so you'll find it in non-fiction, under C for Cameroon, obviously.´

`Will it be safe inside a book?´ asked Zoot.

`It's safer than a safe,´ answered Peaches

with a grin. `That book's been in the library for nine years, and no one's ever borrowed it. See you on Monday.´

`She really is Awesome,´ said Zoot, watching as my best friend headed for the library.

`She's as **Dull And Boring** as the rest of you,´ said Bobby, pushing past us and going into school.

When the bell rang for lunch, Zoot and I went to get the comic straight away. We looked along all the books in non-fiction by authors beginning with C, but *The Lives of British Prime Ministers* wasn't there. We began to search the titles in each section, and soon found it under D for David.

`It's not like Peaches to put a book in the

wrong place,' I said, flicking through the pages.

The comic wasn't inside.

'Nooooooooooooo!' we cried together.

We began furiously searching through all the big books, and throwing them on a table nearby. The mountain of books grew quickly, but we couldn't find the comic in any of them.

'Maybe she thought Bobby Bragg overheard us talking about it, and decided to hide it somewhere else,' I suggested. 'The trouble is we can't get in touch to ask her where it is.'

'We'll just have to wait until she gets back on Monday,' said Zoot, frowning.

Just then, Miss Wilkins opened the door. The teacher stared at the books scattered across the table and spilling on to the floor.

'What on earth do you two think you're doing?' she snapped. 'Look at this mess. You've ruined all Peaches' hard work. Playtime detention on Monday and lose five SHINE TIME points each. Now tidy it up!'

She looked at me and shook her head sadly. 'What would Peaches say?'

'She'd say, "Make sure you put them back in alphabetical order," miss,' I replied.

CHAPTER 10

BLACKMAIL!

I didn't see Zoot over the weekend because he was busy helping out on the set of his dad's movie. I was back to my usual **Dull And Boring** weekend.

Algy had got it into his brain that he only ever lost at chess when I wasn't watching him, so I spent the whole of Saturday watching him play for England. I'm a **BRILLIANT** lucky chess mascot, because he won all his matches!

Then on Sunday I had to stand for hours in a park in the rain with the rest of my family, trying to look like I was enjoying myself as the twins performed at a special charity dance-athon show. The Mystery of the Disappearing *Doomsday Scrolls* comic was on my mind all the time. Even sharing a raspberry-ripple ice cream and reading one of my other **Agent Q** comics with Constanza on Sunday night didn't cheer me up. I just couldn't concentrate.

On Monday morning, I saw Zoot standing by the school gates. Constanza had barely stopped the car before I was out of the door and dashing towards him. We waited for Peaches, looking for her in the crush of chattering grown-ups and shouting kids pouring into the playground, but as the bell rang to start the day she still hadn't arrived. We found out why when we sat down for registration.

'I was hoping that Peaches would be here this morning to tell us all about her trip to count sheep on the Porkney Isles,' said Miss Wilkins.
'But unfortunately they've had gale-force winds up there, and she's stranded on the island. The ferry bringing the volunteers

back to the mainland was cancelled and we don't know when she'll be home. How adventurous!'

'Oh no!' moaned Zoot. 'We'll just have to look through more books at breaktime.'

'We can't,' I said. 'We've got playtime detention, and at lunch we've got to get the field ready for Sports Day this afternoon.'

'I have to find my comic,' said Zoot. 'I'm in Big Trouble if I don't. My dad paid a thousand dollars for it.'

My jaw dropped. 'Mum and Dad wouldn't pay a penny for one of my comics. They just don't get why I like them so much.'

Zoot sighed and opened his work tray under the table. There was an envelope sitting on top of his books. He opened it and pulled out a photograph.

'Look! The comic wasn't lost – it was stolen!' hissed Zoot. 'And we both know who did it.'

'But we can't prove it,' I replied. 'That could be anyone's hand. What are we going to do?'

'I can't let him shred the comic,' Zoot said with a sigh. 'I'll have to let him beat me.'

Miss Wilkins called Bobby Bragg up to do his **SHOW AND TELL.** Usually, we did our little talks on our own, but this time Bobby and Toby Hadron stood up together.

'All this week I've been running fast,' said Bobby. 'And with Toby's help I'm getting faster every day.'

'How interesting!' said Miss Wilkins. 'I just hope you don't blow up like his Primordial Soup did.'

Toby's face reddened as a little bubble of chuckling burst from the rest of the class. 'Er . . . Bobby's my new science project,' he said hurriedly. 'I've put together a special training programme based on the one used by Hussein Bullitt, the world's fastest man.' He grinned. 'But mine's better. It's a strict diet of top-secret high-energy food and drinks, a tough course of scientifically proven exercises and carefully monitored sprints. I've been checking Bobby's heart, pulse, sweat, breathing and brainwaves to make sure he's in tip-top shape.'

'How scientific!' said Miss Wilkins. 'Is it working?'

Toby showed us a chart with a jagged red

line slowly moving upwards. `As you can see,´ he replied. `Bobby's times for the sprint are getting better each day.´

While Toby talked, Bobby stood still, never once taking his eyes off Zoot, who glared back at his cousin. The rest of the class was silent. The tension in the air was like lightning crackling between the two of them.

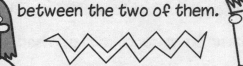

`But will Bobby be fast enough today?´ said Jamie Ryder, breaking the uncomfortable silence.

Toby opened his mouth to answer, but Bobby interrupted him.

`I'll win,´ he said.

The other kids did their presentations,

but no one was really paying any attention, and there weren't many questions. Everyone's mind was on the Big Race.

Miss Wilkins called my name. 'What have you done this weekend, Oliver?' she asked.

I stared at Bobby, looking so pleased with himself, and thought about Toby trying to make Bobby unbeatable. I had to let the class know that Bobby was up to no good, and I also had to let Zoot know what I thought he should do about it.

WHAT IF...

'When Captain Common Sense and I had disarmed the Megabot, we thought the world was safe,' I began. 'Captain Common Sense had sensibly decided to take a holiday. But we should have known that the Show-off wouldn't give up without a fight.'

'I can feel another playtime detention
winging your way, Oliver,' said Miss Wilkins.

'You're supposed to be telling us about something you did over the weekend.'

'Sorry, miss,' I replied. 'But this is serious! The Show-off-bot had armour plating that would stand up to anything; and laser-cannons in his chest that blasted lethal, mega-neutronic fizzer particles; and X-ray eyes that could see through buildings; and hydraulic fingers that could crush concrete, and snap through steel.'

Millie Dangerfield yelped like a frightened puppy. `The D.O.P.E.S. are our only hope!'

Jamie Ryder cheered. `Go, **DAB**MAN! Go, Megabot!'

`Go, playtime detention!' added Miss Wilkins with a smile.

`The two super-**robots** faced each other across the ruins of the city . . .' I went on.

I thought about Peaches, stuck on her windy island. **WHAT IF** . . . it wasn't a gale that was stopping her coming home? **WHAT IF** she'd been captured . . .

`The Show-off-bot pointed to the roof of a building,' I went on. The Boffin and the Spell Queen had taken Captain Common Sense hostage!

'The Show-off can't win,' said Leon Curley.

'Do something, **DAB***MAN*!' cried Millie Dangerfield.

'What could I do?' I replied. 'If the Show-off won, he would rule the world. If Megabot won,

then my partner would end up as Common Sense
Soup. I looked at the Captain. She frowned and
shook her head...'

A tense silence gripped my classmates. My
heart thudded in my chest as I stared at Zoot
and said...

I'm sorry, Captain! Megabot . . . destroy the Show-off-bot!

THE MEGABOT TEARS HIS METALLIC OPPONENT TO PIECES AND LIFTS THE SHOW-OFF FROM THE WRECKAGE.

YOUR SHOW-OFF DAYS ARE OVER! I'M TAKING YOU TO JAIL!

AND CAPTAIN COMMON SENSE IS DOOMED! CUT THE ROPE!

THE BOFFIN SLICES THROUGH THE ROPE . . .

HA-HA-HAAAAAAA!

`Captain!' I yelled. I jumped in my rocket ship

and landed on the rooftop in less than a minute.

I raced over to the vat of bubbling, seething

soup . . . but there was nothing to be seen. Captain Common Sense had dissolved in the evil brew. She was gone.´

´Nooooooooooooooo!´ wailed Millie and Leon.

´I was devastated,´ I said, staring at Zoot. ´But the Captain was right: evil must be defeated at any cost.´

Zoot stared back for a moment, then looked down at the table in front of him.

The rest of the class watched in silence as I walked back to my seat. They knew this was more than just one of my stories.

´How sad,´ said Miss Wilkins, blinking her eyes and giving a little sniff. ´But you're right, Oliver: we must *never* give in to bullies.´

Zoot barely spoke for the rest of the

morning. I'd said all I could, so I left him alone to think about it.

At break, I sat in class with Miss Wilkins and wrote down my story, while Zoot was in the library making sure all the books we'd pulled from the shelves were tidy.

'Ollie, is there something going on between you and Zoot and Bobby?' she asked.

It was a good thing I wasn't connected to Toby's Ping Pong Machine.

'No, miss,' I answered.

That afternoon, the school field was packed with kids, teachers and parents. My mum was doing brain operations, and my dad had taken Algy to London to take part in the National Junior

Brainbox Competition, but Constanza had come
to cheer me on.

'*Bravo*, Oliver!' she called as I came fourth
in the egg and spoon race. 'You
did not finish at the end!'

'No, Constanza, I didn't
come last.'

The Big Race was the final event, and just
before it was about to start I ran over to speak
to Zoot.

'What are you going to do?' I asked.

My friend carried on warming up. 'I can't
let him shred the comic,' he replied, looking away
from me. 'I'm gonna lose.'

'But you're giving in to blackmail!' I said.

Zoot spun round, and leaned in close to
my face. He had tears in his eyes, and his voice

trembled with rage. 'If it was *your* copy, would *you* let him destroy it?'

I couldn't answer him. I didn't know what to say.

Zoot's shoulders sagged. He took a deep breath and sighed. 'It doesn't matter,' he said, turning away and heading for the starting line. 'It's just a stupid race.'

All the other events had stopped as kids, parents and teachers crowded along the straight running track to watch the Big Race. As the runners lined up, all the noise and **excitement** of the afternoon had suddenly gone. A weird, tense silence gripped the crowd.

I stood about halfway down the track, standing on tiptoes to see over the heads of the people in front. I saw Bobby Bragg smirking as he said something to Zoot. My friend didn't reply, but stood completely still, hands on his hips, staring down the track.

'On your marks!' shouted the head teacher.

The runners crouched down.

'Get set...'

They leaned forward.

'Go!'

The spectators let out a deafening roar as the runners leaped away from the start. In just a few paces, Bobby Bragg had already

edged ahead. As they reached halfway, Zoot was lagging behind even the rest of the runners, never mind Bobby, who was a good couple of metres in front.

I watched them rush away from me towards the finishing line. I jumped up and down, desperately trying to see, but the bobbing heads and waving arms of those in front got in the way. I heard a huge cheer from the spectators near the finish as the winner broke through the tape, so I pushed my way out of the crowd, and hurried to the far end of the field.

The runners stood or knelt on the ground trying to get their breath back. Bobby Bragg leaned over with his hands on his knees, taking deep breaths and staring at Zoot, who had collapsed to the floor, his body shaking with what seemed to be deep, painful sobs. Two teachers fussed around him, trying to get him to his feet.

I burst through the crowd and dashed over to help them. `Are you OK, Zoot?´

`Did . . . Bobby . . . win?´ he gasped.

`I don´t know. I couldn´t see.´

Miss Wilkins had been in charge of announcements all afternoon, and now her voice boomed across the field from the loudspeaker nearby.

`How **exciting**!´ she trilled. `The winner of the boys´ Big Race . . .´ She was interrupted by a deafening, screeching whine from the speaker, which made us all wince in pain. She fiddled with a button on her microphone.

'Oops, sorry about that!' she said. 'Now, where was I? Oh yes, the winner of the boys' Big Race, and the fastest boy in school, is . . .' Miss Wilkins paused a few seconds to torture us all even more. 'Zoot Zipparolli!'

There was an enormous cheer as kids and teachers surged around us to pat Zoot on the back.

He closed his eyes and hung his head. 'I couldn't let him win, Ollie. Maybe he'll see I won fair and square, and give me the comic back.'

'You don't know Bobby Bragg,' I said, searching for him in the crowd. My stomach twisted. 'I can't see him – he's gone!'

'The library!' gasped Zoot. 'Go, Ollie! You've got to stop him!'

173

I scampered through the crowd of kids and parents milling around, but they seemed to be deliberately getting in my way and slowing me down. I dodged and pushed my way across the field, until at last I broke clear and sprinted towards the school.

The door into the changing rooms should have been open, but someone had locked it.

`Bragg!'

I raced round to the main entrance, and pressed the buzzer. There was no one in the office to let me in! I kept my finger on the button, and hammered on the door. Eventually, one of the reception ladies strolled down the corridor with a cup of tea in her hand. She sauntered up to the door and opened it.

`What's the rush?' she said as I dashed past

her and zoomed down the corridor towards the library.

I crashed through the door and headed straight for the shredder. A small plastic carrier bag sat on top of Peaches' desk, right next to the machine. Gasping for breath, I opened the bag and saw bits of **Agent Q** on some of the long strips of paper stuffed inside.

The comic was hamster-bedding.

'Noooooooooooooooo!'

CHAPTER 11

A SENSIBLE ENDING

The library door burst open and Zoot charged in, his gold first-place medal swinging round his neck.

`Did he shred it?´ he asked, breathing heavily.

I held out the bag towards him, and nodded.

Zoot took it from me. `I didn´t think he´d *actually* do it. I didn´t realize how much he wanted to win.´

'We told you: Bobby always has to win,' I said. 'Shall we tell Miss Wilkins?'

'What's the point?' replied Zoot, running his fingers through the pile of shredded paper. 'We can't prove it was him. It's our word against his.'

The library door opened again, and Peaches breezed in.

'Did I miss the Big Race?' she asked. 'Who won?'

'I won the race,' replied Zoot, holding up the bag of shreddings. 'But I lost my comic.'

We quickly told Peaches what had happened while she'd been away.

'Bobby must have overheard me telling you where I was going to hide it,' she said, 'then sneaked in and stolen it when I wasn't there.´

    `So *that's* why we found the big book in the
D section,´ I said. `Bobby must have thought it
went in D for David.´

    Peaches went behind the desk and pulled
out a large brown envelope from the bottom of
a drawer. `Just before I left for the Porkney
Isles, I made a copy of the comic.´ She handed it
to Zoot. `I was going to ask you if it was OK to
give the copy to Ollie as a surprise present after
you'd gone, but I think you should have it now. I
know it's not the same, but . . .´

    Zoot pulled *Agent Q and the
Doomsday Scrolls* from the envelope and his
mouth dropped open. It was an amazing copy.

    `It's as good as the real thing!´ I said.

    `I know. I couldn't tell the difference,´

admitted Peaches. 'I even bought the same kind
of paper . . .' She stopped and frowned at Zoot.
'Why are you sniffing it?'

'Page nine smells of strawberries!' he
said, a massive grin spreading across his face.

'Last year, I dribbled a bit
of strawberry milkshake
on it, and the smell never
went away.'

'The copier's good,' said
Peaches, 'but it's not that good.'

'Which means . . .' I said.

'It's the real comic!' we cried together.

'Which means . . .' I repeated.

'Bobby shredded the fake!'

Zoot decided to borrow David Cameroon's
big boring book to keep the comic in, so

Peaches stamped it and we headed back to the classroom. Our classmates let out a huge cheer when Zoot walked through the door. He smiled and took a deep bow.

Bobby Bragg scowled at him, but then the corner of his mouth turned up in a slight smile when he saw the plastic bag of shredded paper in Zoot's hand.

`Well done, Peaches,´ said Miss Wilkins when she saw my friend was back. `You escaped from the stormy island.´

Millie Dangerfield tugged at my sleeve. `Bobby Bragg just told me that Captain Common Sense really had been turned into soup, and that the Show-off had escaped and was going to make an army of **robots** to destroy the world. Is it true?´

I was just about to answer, when Miss Wilkins said, `We've got ten minutes until home-time, Oliver. Why don't you tell everyone the end of your fib – I mean your story.´

`But it's not **SHOW AND TELL** time, miss,´ I said.

`It doesn't matter,´ she replied. `I think we'd all like you to tell us what finally happened.´

As everyone settled down in their seats, I thought about all the twists and surprises that had happened today. There was no way I could make up a better story than that! But then I had an idea. **WHAT IF . . .**

I grabbed the plastic bag of shredded comic from Zoot's hand.

`The Show-off was safely locked up behind bars,´ I began.

I glanced over at Bobby Bragg, and saw him frown and lean forward as what I was saying sank into his brain.

'So don't worry, Millie,' I said. 'The Show-off

has been beaten again. He lost the Battle of the Bots, and only destroyed a *fake* Captain Common Sense, not the real one. It was a close call, but the D.O.P.E.S. have saved the world again!´

Millie and Leon cheered.

`And the Show-off knows that whatever happens,´ I continued, `the Megabot will always be there . . . watching him night and day!´

`How reassuring!´ laughed Miss Wilkins, who obviously had no idea what my story was really about.

Bobby knew though. His eyes boiled with anger when I strolled past him on my way back to join Zoot and Peaches, and casually dropped the bag containing the shredded comic in his lap. As he glowered at us, Zoot held up the real comic for him to see.

The bell rang for home-time, and the classroom was filled with the sound of scraping chairs and chattering kids. Bobby flung the plastic bag in the bin, and stormed out of the door.

Peaches, Zoot and I grinned at each other, and high-fived.

`Go, D.O.P.E.S. Go!'

CHAPTER 12

CRITIC

Filming had finished on Mr Zipparolli's film, and he invited me, Peaches and both our families to the end-of-shoot party. It was also an engagement party, as George and Ritzy had announced to the world at last that they were getting married.

To get in the house, we had to walk through a scrum of noisy, excited photographers, held back by a handful of policemen on each side of the door. They pushed and shoved and shouted, and their cameras went *flash-flash-flash-flash-flash* as we hurried past. I was glad to get inside.

'No wonder George and Ritzy didn't want the secret to get out!' said Peaches as we escaped into the hallway.

I looked back through the door, and saw Emma and Gemma posing for the photographers.

`We're at the Royal Ballet School,´ said Emma.

`You spell my name with a "G",´ said Gemma, making sure they got her name right.

I saw Bobby Bragg in the crowd of people at the party, but he hadn't bothered us since the day of the race, and kept out of our way all evening.

When I introduced the twins to George Looney, they went as red as the villainous Strawberry Sisters in *Agent Q and the MILKSHAKE MANGLERS*, and made tiny, strangled squeaking sounds. In fact, the place was stuffed with film stars, all there to celebrate the engagement, and Emma and Gemma just sat and stared at celebrities all night, and barely said a word. It was awesome!

Algy found out that Ritzy Savoy was a chess champion when she was at school, so he challenged her to a game on the giant chess board in the garden. (Algy lost, but I think he was just being polite.)

Constanza prattled away in Italian all night with Mr Zipparolli's Italian chef, and swapped special meatball recipes with him. I kept hearing words like, *`Bellisima!'*, *`Magnifico!'*, *`Mama mia!'* and `gas mark six'.

After talking to Peaches' mum and dad, Mr Zipparolli decided he was going to make a film about the Sheep Counters of Porkney:

`A tale of romance, danger and woolly jumpers.´

Mum and Dad were overjoyed, because Zoot's mum asked my dad to design their new house in Bermuda! How cool is that?

`Well done, Ollie,´ whispered Dad. `You've made some very important friends.´

At the end of the party, we made ourselves comfortable in the soft chairs of Mr Zipparolli's private cinema, and watched a rough version of the new film. It was awesome, with car chases, and fantastic spy gadgets and explosions. When it was over, Zoot's dad said, `It still needs a lot of work and music and so on, but what do you think?´

`It makes the James Pond movies look like Mary Bobbins!´ I said, and everyone laughed.

`That's what I'm gonna put on all the

posters!' laughed Mr Zipparolli.

Mum whispered in my ear. 'Well done, Oliver,' she said. (TWO 'well dones' in one day! That's *almost* Super And Special!). 'Maybe you're going to be a **BRILLIANT** film critic,' she added.

Zoot's mum leaned over. 'Actually, Ollie is a very good storyteller,' she said seriously. 'I think he might be a **BRILLIANT** author one day.'

'*Really?*' said Mum and Dad together.

They wouldn't have been more surprised if Mrs Zipparolli had told them I wasn't their son but an alien **robot** from the planet Blooporia-trumbob 5. They stared at me for ages with looks of flabbergast all over their faces. (It wasn't pretty.) I shuffled my feet, looked away and coughed nervously. I felt like a bug under a microscope.

'Maybe we should send you on a writing course?' said Mum.

'And get you some books on creative writing,' added Dad.

'Big ones, please,' I said.

'Big enough to hide your comics in, I hope,' whispered Zoot.

When it was time to leave, Zoot took me and Peaches to one side. He handed me a copy of *Agent Q and the Doomsday Scrolls.*

'Pea, you made another one for me,' I said. 'Thanks.'

'No, Ollie,' she replied. 'I made another copy for *Zoot.*'

Zoot smiled. 'This is the one that smells of

strawberries,' he said. 'Ollie, you're the best pal I've ever had. I want you to have the real one.'

'I . . . But . . . What . . .' I stammered. 'Are you sure?'

He nodded. 'It's yours. Now you've got the full set.'

'Wow, thanks.'

'Promise you'll stay in touch, Zoot?' asked Peaches.

'Are you kidding?' he replied. 'You've not seen the last of me. After all, I'm a D.O.P.E.!'

As we turned to leave, I bumped into Bobby Bragg. He looked at the comic, and then at me. I knew what he was thinking:

STEVE HARTLEY

JOIN DANNY AS HE ATTEMPTS TO SMASH A LOAD OF MADCAP RECORDS

VISIT THE GOBSTOPPERS WEBSITE FOR

AUTHOR NEWS · BONUS CONTENT
VIDEOS · GAMES · PRIZES . . .
AND MORE!